Riley, Kylie and Smiley

Malachy Doyle

Illustrated by
Fran Evans

PONT READALONE

First Impression—2002

ISBN 1 84323 118 2

© text: Malachy Doyle
© illustrations: Fran Evans

This volume is published with the support of the
Arts Council of Wales.

Printed in Wales at
Gomer Press, Llandysul, Ceredigion SA44 4QL

To Aberdyfi crabbers,
one and all

Chapter 1

Riley goes Crabbing

'A fine day for crabbing!' said Riley, springing out of bed. He threw some clothes on his outside, some food in his inside, grabbed his bucket and his crabline and off he scooted, down Copperhill Street to the butcher's.

'Morning, Mr. Roberts,' said Riley, gasping. 'Have you any good crabbing meat?'

'I have, indeed, young Riley,' said the butcher. 'Only the best for you. That'll be twenty pence.'

And he fetched him a bag of his very best fattybits.

Riley was the first to arrive on the jetty, so he raced to his favourite spot, right up at the end, where the water below was deep, green and murky – a perfect home for crabs. He opened his butcher bag, found the meatiest bit there was, and hooked it onto his line.

'Only the best, my little crabbies!' he said, letting out the line and tossing the weight, the hook and the meat into the water. Then he waited and he waited, for the secret is to wait, and while he was waiting he sang his very own crab-catching song.

'Prowling, prowling on the seabed,
Goes the hungry crab.
Gets a whiff of Riley's meat,
And grab it, crab, grab!' he sang.

And when he pulled on the line, he could tell
that they had. Grabbed, that is. Crabs, that is.

Then quietly, smoothly, Riley drew them in – as gently as possible, so as not to alarm them, not to disturb them, not to rattle them off the line.

And there they were – three big ones, all clutching and pinching and munching away, getting well stuck in to Mr. Roberts's fattybits.

Well, there were three big ones when Riley started to pull on the line. But as every good crabber knows, three on the line and three in the bucket are a deeply different thing.

For the first crab let go as soon as it left the safety of the green and murky water and felt the cold, threatening air of the human world.

And the second dropped off at just about the halfway mark, when he suddenly sensed he was bound for the bucket.

But the biggest and best and greediest crab, determined not to lose all that yummy scrummy butchermeat, clung on, all the way up to the top of the jetty, all the way up and over.

A shake and a plop and into the bucket, into the bucket you go.

'That's one, and counting,' said Riley, to no one in particular. And he checked his meat, checked the time and tossed his line back into the sea.

'Morning, Kylie!' said Riley, smiling up at his friend, who'd just arrived. 'Half past nine and the day's nearly over! The early crabber catches the crab, and I'd say you've a lot of catching up to do!'

'Why, how many have you got?' asked Kylie, peering into Riley's blue bucket to do a quick count. 'Twelve!' she said, deeply impressed, and unable to hide her surprise and annoyance.

'Fifteen, actually,' said Riley, correcting her.

But it turned out they were both wrong, for at that very moment the biggest and best and greediest crab clambered up and onto the backs of the others, hooked a claw on the edge of the bucket, and levered itself over and out.

'Sorry, fourteen,' said Riley. 'Clever trick, there, Mr. Crab. I think I need a higher-sided bucket.'

And Kylie smiled too, as the Great Escaper scuttled away to the edge of the jetty and toppled back into the water. Splash, home to the bubbles and fish!

'One less for me to catch, for me to catch up!' said Kylie, grinning.

And she stuck a big bit of juicy red meat on her hook, lay face down on the jetty, fixed a look of great seriousness on her face, and the race was on.

Chapter 2

The Race is On

'Prowling, prowling on the seabed,
Goes the hungry crab.
Gets a whiff of Riley's meat,
And grab it, crab, grab!' muttered Riley,
under his breath. Singing his secret weapon.

'Stop humming, Riley,' said Kylie, deep in
concentration. 'You're putting me off.'

'I'm not humming, I'm singing.'

'Well, stop singing, then.'

Silence, but for the roar of the jet-skis, the
squawk of the seagulls, and the yelling of noisy
toddlers on the beach.

'Anyway, what were you singing?' said
Kylie, looking up.

'I'm not telling.'

'What do you mean you're not telling?'

'I'm just not. That's what.'

'What's what?'

'That is.'

It's lucky the crabs started biting again, or Kylie and Riley might have fallen out, big time.

Bite, bite, fourteen to one.

Bite, bite, fifteen to four.

Bite, bite, fifteen to seven.

And bite, bite, sixteen to ten.

Kylie was catching up!

'S'not fair,' said Riley, grumpily. 'They've nibbled off my meaty bits, and all I'm left with is the fat. Can I borrow a piece of yours, Kylie?'

'Borrow?' said Kylie, giving him a look. 'What do you mean, borrow? Do you think I'd want my lump of best butchermeat back once your nasty crabs have slobbered all over it?'

'Your meat's no better than mine,' replied Riley, crossly, 'for it comes from the same place. And if my crabs are nasty, then so are yours. Just give me a piece, Kylie, and stop being moody!'

'Who are you calling moody?' said Kylie, scowling. 'There's no way you're getting anything now, Riley. This is war!'

'All's fair in war and crabbing,' said a soothing voice.

They looked around, at a pair of tidy trainers.

They looked up, past bony knees, ironed shorts and a clean today T-shirt. And there they saw the friendly face of Smiley, towering above them.

'Hiya, Smiley,' said Riley.

'How's it going, mate?' said Kylie.

'Oh, fair dinkum,' said Smiley. 'Whatever that means.'

And he sat down between them and watched the war.

Only it wasn't a war anymore, now that Smiley was there.

Kylie even reached into her bag, leaned across and passed Riley one of her best bits of meat. Smiley has that effect, sometimes.

He brought them luck, too, for Riley's next haul was three crabs, and Kylie's was four.

So the battle was raging at nineteen to fourteen when, 'Wow!' said Riley and 'Yuk!' said Kylie.

The two friends peered over the edge, and there, wriggling like a wombat at the end of Riley's line was a thing. A wriggly, jiggly, ugly thing.

Not a crab. Definitely not a crab.

'What is it?' asked Kylie, nervously.

'I haven't a clue,' answered Riley. 'But it's long and ugly, whatever it is.'

'A bit like you, then,' said Smiley, laughing. And he leaned out, over the side of the jetty, to take a good look.

Chapter 3

Smiley and the Watersnake

'It can't be!' cried Smiley. 'I don't believe it, but it is!'

'Is what?' said Kylie and Riley, together.

'A watersnake!'

'A watersnake?' said Riley, still drawing in his line, but a lot more slowly, now.

Riley wasn't too sure he really wanted to come face to face with a watersnake, you see. In fact, he was even shaking the line a bit, accidentally on purpose, which is something a good Aberdyfi crabber never does. Not enough for Smiley to notice, of course, but maybe, hopefully, just enough for the wiggly jiggly ugly thing to get the message and plop off, back to where it came from, back to the unknown depths.

'What's a watersnake, Smiley?' Kylie asked.

'Whatever it is,' said Riley, with by this time a severe case of the jitters, 'I don't like the look of it. Not one little bit.'

'Actually, you're right to be nervous . . .' said Smiley, reaching out and taking over Riley's line. Who was more than happy to let it go.

'For it's a particularly ferocious creature, extremely rare in these parts,' continued Smiley, with a grin. 'A particularly ferocious South American creature, with an extraordinarily ferocious BITE!'

And with one final flick of the wrist he pulled the wriggly, jiggly slimy thing up over the edge of the jetty and dangled it in the air, right in front of poor Kylie's nose.

Who shrieked, dropped her line into the water and ran.

Smiley stood there, laughing. And laughing.

But, unfortunately, there was no one to laugh with, which rather spoiled the fun of it all, because Kylie was gone, wham, bam, disappeared, and suddenly Riley was nowhere to be seen, either. Vanished. Scooted off. Away.

'*A watersnake, a watersnake, a nasty, horrible watersnake!*' sang Smiley, running up and down the jetty, dangling the slimy wriggly thing between his bony fingers, and generally getting highly over-excited.

'*Come out, come out, for goodness sake,*

And get a bite from the watersnake!' he cried, quite carried away with the success of his little trick. Laughing loud enough for three, just to prove it really was funny in case anyone might doubt it.

Mind you, despite all his dancing he managed to keep the wriggly jiggly slimy thing well away from his tidy trainers, his ironed shorts, and his clean-today T-shirt. For it doesn't pay to get too mucky, now does it? Not if you're a Smiley. Not if you can avoid it, anyway.

'Come out, come out, wherever you are!' he called to his friends. 'I'm only pretending. It's not a watersnake at all – it's only a sand eel! A wriggly, jiggly sand eel!'

And he tossed it back in the water.

'A sand eel!' cried Kylie, stomping out from behind the great stack of lobster pots, banging across the jetty and kicking Smiley a gentle but firm tap on the shin. 'It's nothing but a sand eel!' And then she began to giggle.

They wriggled and they giggled, they giggled and they wriggled, and they were still at it, laughing, that is, when Riley reappeared with a Triple Scoop Sugar Cone Fruits of the Forest Honey Ice, complete with a Milk Chocolate Flakey thing.

And to show there were no major hard feelings, he let them both have a lick.

But to show Smiley, nevertheless, that he, Riley, was just a teenchy-weenchy bit fed-up with the trick his so-called friend had played on them . . .

To draw Smiley's attention to the fact that there was funny and there was funny and that scaring the pants off Kylie and Riley WASN'T VERY FUNNY . . .

To let it be known, in a gentle sort of a way, that there was a fine line between having a laugh and going too far and that this was most definitely one of those occasional but very annoying times when Smiley managed to cross it . . .

Yes, to show Smiley all of that and more, Riley let Kylie have a bite of his flake. That yummy, scrummy, melt-in-your-mouth, deliciously chocolate flake.

Not Smiley.

Just Kylie.

Chapter 4

Riley, Kylie, Smiley and the Sandboy

'How come she gets a bit of flake and I don't?' said Smiley.

'Just because,' said Riley, licking the last of his Triple Scoop.

'Just because what?' said Smiley.

'Just because I say so and it's mine,' answered Riley, starting on his Sugar Cone.

'How about a bite of your Sugar Cone, then?' said Smiley.

'Sorry,' said Riley, smiling. 'It seems to have all gone!'

'I'll get you for that!' said Smiley, springing up from the jetty.

So off went Riley, like a greyhound on a racetrack.

And off went Smiley, like a hundred-metre sprinter.

Round and past the Yacht Club, in and out of
boats, running, hiding, never catching, down
and onto the beach.

Jump!

Straight onto a little boy's sandcastle. A little boy with a suddenly crumpled face.

'Oh, I'm really sorry,' said Smiley, introducing himself. And he was, too. Sorry, that is. For even though Smiley liked nothing better than playing tricks on people his own age, he wasn't a sandcastle stomper. He didn't pick on little ones.

'Would you like me to help you dig a hole, little boy?' he said, hoping to put a smile back on the crumpled face. 'I'm very good at digging holes.'

'Yep peas,' said the sandboy, suddenly wide-eyed and watching.

So Smiley borrowed the little boy's spade and began some serious digging.

And soon Kylie came to see what was going on, and joined in, with her bare hands.

And soon Riley realised that no one was chasing him any more so there wasn't a whole lot of point running on and ever onwards. So back he came, all puffing and panting and gasping for breath. And he joined in too.

So they dug and they dug, Smiley, Kylie and Riley, and soon they'd dug a GREAT BIG HOLE.

'Would you like to get into the hole, little boy?' said Smiley, and the little fellow, boggle-eyed, looked over at his Mum, who was sitting in a deck-chair, reading a magazine. And watching, too, of course, out of the corner of her eye, like Mums do.

Mum nodded.

So the little sandboy jumped down into the hole, splat. And when he got back up onto his feet, brushed the sand off his two pudgy knees, and stood in the hole, upright, it was so deep that he couldn't even see over the top.

'Weh a you, Miley?' said he, not sure whether to be thrilled or terrified.

'Here I am!' said Smiley, and with a blood-curdling yell he jumped over the hole, to a shriek of laughter from the sandboy below.

'Weh a you, Wiley?' said the sandboy, for by this time Riley and Kylie had told him their names, too.

'Here I am!' said Riley, throwing himself flat on the sand, next to the hole, and popping his head out, 'Boo!'

Another shriek of laughter from the little man.

Then 'Weh a you, Ky?' said he, giggling.

'Here I am,' said Kylie, and she sprang down into the hole, right next to the sandboy. Who screamed even louder with delight.

Chapter 5

Kylie and the Sandboy's Bucket

And then Riley and Smiley started digging a channel to the sea. The tide was coming in, so that as soon as they reached it the water began to pour down the channel and into the hole.

'Right, that's enough water,' said Kylie, when it was up to everyone's knees (and up to the sandboy's tummy. At which point a large hand, the hand of an ever-watchful Mum, reached into the hole and plucked him to safety).

So the three friends all stood in the hole, blocked off the channel and began to make a great wall of wet sand all the way round, to stop the sea from coming any further.

And they were watched by the sandboy, who by now was sitting up on the jetty, stuffing his face with a Single Scoop Raspberry Ripple (no flake).

'Gun ga weh,' said the sandboy to his mother.

'I'd say you're right, love,' said his Mum, smiling. 'They're going to get very wet.'

'Icky tik,' said the sandboy.

'You're right about that, too,' said his Mum, fetching a tissue out of her bag to wipe the sticky ice-cream from her little boy's tummy. 'It's melting, love – you'd better eat it up, quick!'

Meanwhile, back down by the sea, the tide had come in, all around the hole. But the three friends hadn't given up. Riley, Kylie and Smiley were still there, baling out the water with the sandboy's bucket and building up the walls with wet sand.

Then, 'Abandon ship!' said Captain Kylie, at last, and they left the hole in the hands of the ocean.

Running and splashing, back up the beach.
'Ukkit, bukkit,' said the sandboy, pointing. But his mother didn't look where he was pointing, for she only had eyes for her clever little boy, who'd just added a fine new word to his limited vocabulary.

And the three friends were too far away to hear his warning, of course. But by some strange coincidence Kylie turned back at that very moment to look at the sea, and saw the sandboy's yellow bucket, which they'd left behind in the hole.

Only by now there was no hole left. Nothing but the Irish Sea. And the sandboy's bucket, bobbing about on the waves.

So Kylie dashed down the beach, waded into the water, up to her middle, and grabbed it.

'Clap, clap,' went the sticky hands of the sandboy, up on the jetty, as Riley, Smiley and a soggy Kylie trekked back up to give him his bucket.

'Anku,' said the sandboy, smiling, as Kylie handed it back to him.

'And thank YOU, little sandboy,' said Riley, 'for lending us your bucket.'

'Ukkit,' said the sandboy, once more. But this time he was pointing at Riley and Kylie's crabbing buckets, up at the far end of the jetty, where they'd left them ages ago.

'Oh, the poor crabs,' said Kylie, suddenly remembering what the morning was supposed to be all about. 'We forgot to put them back in the water!'

So the sandboy's Mum took him by one hand and Kylie took him by the other, and they all marched up to the far end, to have a look in the buckets.

'Wab!' said the sandboy, delightedly. 'Wab, wab!'

So Kylie transferred some of her water and two of her crabs into the sandboy's bucket, and then everyone headed down to the water's edge to release them.

The jolly little sandboy didn't much want to let go of his two crabs so soon after getting them, but Kylie explained that the sea was their home, and that it wasn't really fair to keep them out of it any longer.

'Bye, bye, wab,' said the little fellow, sadly, tipping up his bucket at the same time as Kylie and Riley. And everyone watched in silence as the thirty three crabs crawled, one by one, into the ocean.

'Come down tomorrow morning and you can help us catch some more,' said Riley to the sandboy, to cheer him up. Kylie nodded and Smiley nodded and the sandboy's Mum said yes, they would.

And then Riley, Smiley and a soggy Kylie raced off home for dinner.

From the Author . . .

This book is set in a very real place – Aberdyfi, where I live. In Summer, the wharf is jam-packed full of young crabbers, just like Riley, Kylie and Smiley, dangling their bait in the water and trying to entice the wily crabs into their buckets.

Ice cream, sandcastles, crabbing and Aberdyfi – there's nothing and nowhere to beat it.

Malachy

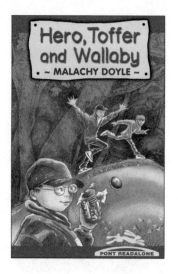

As soon as the bell rings at the end of school, Hero, Toffer and Wallaby make straight for The Den. It's up The Mountain, deep in The Woods, and it's the best place on earth. All day Saturday and Sunday they've been up and down with bits of wood and black plastic. They even carted an old sofa up there, with a little help from Hero's Dad. Finally, with branches across the top, The Den's so well hidden, no one would even know it was there. No one, that is, but for An Intruder.

ISBN 1 85902 845 4 £3.50

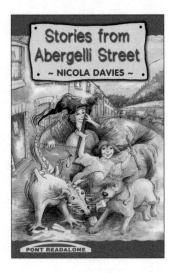

You never know who you'll meet when you walk down
Abergelli Street. Perhaps Cleo will be setting off for the
mountain with her dog, Mr Kidwelly. That would not be
so very surprising. But what about Bwgan the
scarecrow, Uncle Helogan the cold and hungry dragon,
or Caradog the cat, who lodges with Mrs Rhosilli?
Would you like to meet them and find out what dreams
and schemes they have in their heads? In these stories,
you can peek inside every house, eavesdrop on every
amusing conversation and enjoy the wonderful
characters of Abergelli Street.

ISBN 1 84323 075 5   £3.50

Just imagine a house that has been turned into a funfair!
Lauren loves to help out at her Uncle Wil's Wacky Fun
House. But then, one terrible day, Uncle Will confesses
that there's no money to pay the electricity bills to run
the rides. The Fun House has to close and the
marvellous rides will be sold. One thing's for sure, they
won't be selling Gertie and Bertie, their very special
bumper cars – the cars that can set out on adventures all
on their own!
The trouble is, a greedy rival has spotted these
extraordinary dodgems, so are Bertie and Gertie really
safe?

ISBN 1 84323 121 2   £3.50

Being twins, Rhian and Rhys share a birthday – of
course they would – and they also share a very lively
grandmother. Mam-gu is always saying that people
should show plenty of 'oomph'! The bad news for the
twins is that Mam-gu puts an awful lot of oomph into
her knitting – an outrageous amount of oomph, in fact.
What will their birthday presents be this year?
Something knitted, that's for sure. The twins just have
to be brave and open up their fat, lumpy parcels. But
will Rhian and Rhys dare show their friends what Mam-
gu has dreamed up for them this time?

ISBN 1 84323 034 8   £3.50

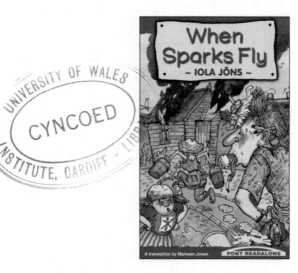

When
Sparks Fly
~ IOLA JÔNS ~

A translation by Mairwen Jones   PONT READALONE

Gwenno loves her father. She loves playing football
with him and going to the woods to explore. What she
doesn't love one little bit is his smoking. Gwenno
absolutely hates cigarettes. She can't stand the smell of
smoke. She loathes the sight of ashtrays and stub-ends.
What on earth can she do to persuade her dad to give
up? She's certainly not short of good ideas, and she has
a friend, Lowri, to help her. But Dad is stubborn, and
Mam is very soft-hearted. She's likely to say, 'Leave
your poor father alone, Gwenno.' Well Gwenno won't
leave him alone, that's for sure. She's determined to ban
the smoking, even if it causes sparks to fly.

ISBN 1 84323 016 X   £3.50